Alfie
all Alone

D1114751

Other titles by Holly Webb

The Snow Bear

The Reindeer Girl

The Winter Wolf

Animal Stories:

Lost in the Snow

Lost in the Storm

Sam the Stolen Puppy

Max the Missing Puppy

Sky the Unwanted Kitten

Timmy in Trouble

Ginger the Stray Kitten

Harry the Homeless Puppy

Buttons the Runaway Puppy

Alone in the Night

Ellie the Homesick Puppy

Jess the Lonely Puppy

Misty the Abandoned Kitten

Oscar's Lonely Christmas

Lucy the Poorly Puppy

Smudge the Stolen Kitten

The Rescued Puppy

The Kitten Nobody Wanted

The Lost Puppy

The Frightened Kitten

The Secret Puppy

The Abandoned Puppy

The Missing Kitten

The Puppy Who was Left Behind

The Kidnapped Kitten

The Scruffy Puppy

The Brave Kitten

The Forgotten Puppy

The Secret Kitten

A Home for Molly

My Naughty Little Puppy:

A Home for Rascal

New Tricks for Rascal

Playtime for Rascal

Rascal's Sleepover Fun

Rascal's Seaside Adventure

Rascal's Festive Fun

Rascal the Star

Rascal and the Wedding

Alfie
all Alone

Holly Webb
Illustrated by Sophy Williams

stripes

For Alice, Max and Georgie

www.hollywebbanimalstories.com

STRIPES PUBLISHING
An imprint of Little Tiger Press
1 The Coda Centre, 189 Munster Road,
London SW6 6AW

A paperback original
First published in Great Britain in 2007

Text copyright © Holly Webb, 2007
Illustrations copyright © Sophy Williams, 2007
Author photograph copyright © Nigel Bird
My Naughty Little Puppy illustration copyright © Kate Pankhurst

ISBN: 978-1-84715-015-8

A CIP catalogue record for this book is available
from the British Library.

Printed and bound in the UK.

20 19 18 17 16 15

Chapter One

"Evie, did you put these in the trolley?" Evie's mum was staring at a packet of rice cakes, looking confused.

"No. Why would I, Mum, they look horrible." Evie made a face. "It was you, don't you remember? You said they might be nice to nibble on when you were feeling sick. But I bet they'll just make you feel even more sick."

Her mum sighed. "You're probably right. She smiled apologetically at the assistant who was waiting for them to pay. "Sorry. I seem to be a bit forgetful at the moment."

The girl smiled back. "That's OK. My sister's pregnant and she locked herself out of the house twice last week. How long until the baby's due?"

"Another nine weeks." Evie's mum sighed. "The time just seems to be creeping past at the moment." She patted her enormous tummy.

"Mum, can I go and look at the noticeboard?" Evie asked. She was getting a bit bored with baby talk. Ever since her mum's bump had begun to show, complete strangers had started talking to them in the street, asking about the baby. They always asked Evie how she felt about having a little brother or sister, and she was sick of having to smile and say she was looking forward to it. She was, but the fussing was starting to get on her nerves. And she had a horrible feeling that it would get a lot worse after the baby arrived.

"Of course you can. Actually, Evie, see if anyone's selling any baby stuff. It would be a good way to find some bargains."

Evie sighed quietly. Honestly, did Mum ever think about anything else? She wandered over to the big board behind the Customer Service point where they put up the advertisements. You could find some really fun things sometimes. Once she'd spotted an advert for a pair of nearly new roller blades that someone had grown out of – she'd been able to afford them with her pocket money, and they were great.

She browsed through vacuum cleaners, lawn mowers, a girl offering to babysit – and then caught her breath in delight. The next ad was larger than some of the others, and it had a photo attached – a basket of the cutest little white dogs, all clambering over each other. One of them was grinning out at Evie, a naughty glint in his eye.

WESTIE PUPPIES READY
FOR HOMES NOW
REASONABLE PRICE
Call Mrs Wilson on 295561

Evie sighed adoringly. That puppy was gorgeous! She had to show him to Mum. She looked back over at the till to see if she was done yet. Her mum was looking round for her, and Evie waved, and then dashed over.

"Come and see! You'll love it. Anyway, you shouldn't be pushing that on your own, Mum, Dad would be really cross." Evie helped her mum with the trolley, giving her a stern glare.

"Dad is a fusspot." Mum chuckled. "What am I looking at?" She stared at the board, trying to work out what

Evie was so excited about. "We're not buying a trampoline, Evie," she said, grinning. "And we definitely don't want a speedboat!"

"No, look, I just wanted you to see this cute photo." Evie pointed out the basket of puppies. "Aren't they sweet?"

"Oh, yes, they're lovely. What sort of dog are they? Westies…" Mum gazed thoughtfully at the photo. "Westies are quite small dogs, aren't they?" she mused quietly.

Evie nodded. "I think Mrs Jackson down the road's got a Westie. You know, Tyson? He's gorgeous."

"Mmmm." Evie's mum nodded. "OK. I suppose you're going to insist on pushing this trolley now, aren't you? Actually, Evie, do you want to go and look at the animal magazines – I have to go to the loo again." She sighed theatrically. "Don't move from the magazines, I'll only be a minute."

As soon as Evie set off, her mum scrabbled hastily in her handbag for a pen. Then she made a note of the name and phone number from the puppy advert on her till receipt, and hurried after Evie.

As they drove home, Evie gazed out of the window, day-dreaming about puppies. She had no idea that her mum was sneaking glances at her every so often. Over the last few weeks, Evie's mum and dad had been worrying about how the new baby was going to affect her. After all, eight was quite old to suddenly have a new baby brother or sister. Evie seemed to be happy about it, but it was difficult to tell. They'd been wondering what they could do to stop her feeling left out, and it was only the day before that Evie's dad had thought of getting her a puppy. Her mum hadn't been too sure.

"Won't it be a lot of hassle, just before the baby comes?" she'd worried.

"We've got a few weeks. And the point is that Evie would be doing all the looking after – it'll give her something to fuss over when we're fussing over the baby." Evie's dad was really enthusiastic. He liked dogs, and he knew Evie would love a puppy.

After all, a puppy had been at the top of her Christmas list for the last three years. Her parents had always said she wasn't quite old enough – mostly because Evie's mum thought having a dog would be a lot of work. But Evie's dad had been trying hard to convince her, so the Westie ad had turned up at the perfect time.

"What are you thinking about, Evie?" Mum asked her, smiling. "You're miles away."

Evie grinned. "Just that lovely dog. I know we can't have a puppy, but if we did, I'd like one just like him…"

Evie's dad got home just in time to help make dinner, and Evie told him about the little white dog as she was setting the table.

"Puppies? For sale now?" he asked thoughtfully.

Evie saw him exchange a glance with her mum and caught her breath, her eyes widening in sudden hope. She looked back and forth between them. Her dad was grinning. "Funny you should spot that ad today, Evie. Your mum and I were talking last night. We've been thinking about getting you a dog and just now seems the right time."

Evie could hardly believe her ears.

"You mean it?" she breathed delightedly.

Mum nodded. "If you think you can

look after a dog properly. It's a big responsibility."

Evie nodded so hard she made her neck ache. "I know, I know. I can!"

Mum smiled. "So, shall I ring the lady with these puppies? You'd like a Westie?"

Evie just gaped at them. She'd wanted a dog for so long, and her parents had always said, "Maybe," and "Perhaps when you're older." Then she suddenly realized what her mum had just said and squeaked, "Yes! Yes, please!"

Evie hardly ate any tea. She watched her parents eating impatiently, and when her dad had swallowed his last mouthful of pasta she snatched the plate away to put in the washing-up.

"Hey! Evie! I was going to have seconds!" He smiled. "OK, OK. Let's put you out of your misery."

Evie waited anxiously while her mum called the number. What if all the puppies had gone? After all, they didn't know how long the advertisement had been up there. She sat on the stair listening to her mum. It was horribly difficult to work out what was going on, but eventually her mum said, "Great. Well, we'll come round tomorrow morning. Thanks!" and then she put the phone down and beamed at Evie.

"I'm getting a puppy!" Evie gasped, jumping up and down in excitement. "I can't believe it! I have to go round and tell Gran!"

Evie's gran lived a couple of streets away, with her own two dogs, Ben the spaniel, and Tigger, who was a greyhound cross with crazy stripes. Evie heard them barking madly as she rang the doorbell. She grinned to herself. She couldn't wait to introduce Ben and Tigger to her new puppy!

"Guess what, guess what!" she gabbled as Gran opened the door. "I'm getting a dog!" She didn't manage to say much after that as Tigger was jumping up and trying to lick her face.

"Down, Tigger! Stop it, silly boy, it's only Evie, you see her every day!" Gran shooed the dogs away and went into the kitchen to put the kettle on. "Darling, did you say you were getting a dog?"

"A puppy! Mum and Dad are giving me a puppy – we're going to pick one out tomorrow morning." Evie sighed blissfully. She wasn't sure she could wait that long.

Gran looked confused. "But ... just before the baby arrives?"

Evie nodded happily. Then she leaned over the table, lowering her voice as though she were telling secrets. "They didn't say, but I think it's to make me feel better about the baby," she explained.

Her grandma nodded thoughtfully. "Well, everyone would understand if you found it difficult, Evie, you know that, don't you?"

"Gran, you know I'm really looking forward to it." Evie laughed. "And now

I'll have a puppy as well!" She beamed at Gran, expecting her to be really excited. But Gran was stirring her tea thoughtfully. "What's the matter?" Evie asked, frowning.

"Nothing, Evie. It's lovely news. It's just…" Gran sipped her tea, thinking what to say. "I'm just wondering if this is the right time. With the baby coming. A new puppy will be a lot of work, you know."

Evie shook her head. "Don't worry. I know about looking after dogs from helping with Ben and Tigger, and Dad knows loads about them too." Evie bent down to scratch Tigger behind his ears, so she didn't see her gran's worried face. "I've wanted a dog for so long! I still can't believe it's really happening!" Evie gave Tigger an excited hug. Tomorrow she was going to meet her own puppy for the first time!

Chapter Two

Evie just couldn't stay in bed the next morning. She usually loved having a lie-in on Saturdays after getting up for school all week, but today she was much too excited. She hardly ate any breakfast either – she just stirred her chocolate cereal in circles till it looked like mud.

"You might as well eat it, you know,

Evie," her mum pointed out, slowly buttering a piece of toast. "We're not going yet. I told Mrs Wilson we'd be there at ten."

"But that's hours away!" Evie wailed.

"Mrs Wilson has to feed the puppies and tidy their run and get everything ready," her mum explained. "We can't go round before then."

"I suppose so," Evie agreed reluctantly. She trailed upstairs, wondering what she was going to do to fill a whole hour before they could leave. Then she had a brainwave. She'd go and look up puppies on the Net, to try and find out about looking after a dog. Evie settled down and before long was busy making notes. By the time her mum called her down, Evie's head was bursting with information about feeding, walking, vaccinations and training. It was a lot to think about. But she knew she could do it!

"Oh, look! He's all shy!" Evie giggled, and stretched out her hand to the fluffy white puppy who was peeping out at her round his mother. He took a step back, then curiosity got the better of him. Tail slowly wagging, he began to sneak forwards to where Evie was sitting on the floor.

"He's a little cutie, that one, probably my favourite," Mrs Wilson said fondly. "I'm going to miss him – he's such a sweet-natured dog."

Mum shook her head. "I don't know
how you can bear to see them go.
They're all so gorgeous." She scratched
the puppy she was cuddling under the
chin, and the little dog snuffled happily
at her fingers.

"Well, this is the last time I'll have to, actually." Mrs Wilson sighed. "Lady and I are getting too old for puppies! We're retiring, aren't we, my special girl?" She patted the puppies' mother, a beautiful snow-white dog with melting brown eyes. "We're going to live by the sea. Lady loves walking along the beach. And getting soaking wet!"

Evie could have sworn that Lady's eyes sparkled naughtily. That was the amazing thing about her and the puppies – they all seemed so bright and intelligent. Then the fluffy little boy puppy suddenly nuzzled at her hand, and she squeaked in delight. She'd been watching Lady and not noticed him creeping up on her.

"He seems to have taken a shine to

you, Evie." Dad laughed, watching the puppy chasing Evie's fingers as she danced her hand up and down.

Evie nodded, and then looked seriously at both Mum and Dad. "Is it really up to me to choose?" she asked worriedly. "I mean, all four of them are wonderful."

"It's a hard job," Dad agreed. "But we can't take them all."

Evie giggled as the little boy puppy mountaineered up her jeans, trying to climb into her lap. She helped him out with a boost under his scrabbly little back paws, and he heaved himself up. Then he turned round four times, gave a great sigh of satisfaction and went to sleep curled up tight in a little white ball.

Evie looked up, her eyes glowing. "This one," she said firmly.

"Mmm, I don't think you had much choice," Dad agreed, smiling. "He's definitely chosen you! Now you just have to think of a name for him."

Evie smiled. "I know what I'm going to call him. His name is Alfie."

Mum and Dad gazed at the little puppy. "That's a lovely name," said Mum. "He looks just like an Alfie."

It was a wrench to leave Alfie behind, but Evie knew she'd see him again the next day. He'd be coming home with them! Now they just had to get everything they needed to look after him. Mrs Wilson had given them a list, and Evie studied it in the car on the way to the pet shop.

"Basket. Food bowl. Water bowl. Collar. Lead. Harness. Chew toys," she muttered.

Dad sighed. "Nearly as bad as the baby," he moaned. "You sure little Alfie doesn't need a cot as well, Evie?"

It was so exciting later that afternoon to see the basket with its smart red cushion waiting in a warm spot in the kitchen, and the collar and lead hanging from one of the coat-hooks in the hallway. Everything was ready for Alfie to come home.

"Oh look, he's found his new basket!"

Evie and her parents were watching Alfie explore his new home. He was trotting around on unsteady paws, sniffing at everything.

"A-choo!" Alfie sneezed and stepped back, shaking his head.

"Ooops!" said Dad. "I didn't know my wellies smelled that bad. Let's leave him to settle in."

That night, Evie sneaked back down to the kitchen after her bedtime to check Alfie was OK. He'd eaten all his dinner and seemed to have made himself at home, but she was worried that he would be lonely, as he was used to sleeping with his mum and his brother and sisters. Alfie had been lying awake. He'd been trying to make sense of all the strange things that had been happening that day. His first car journey; the new house; a new basket to sleep in. And new people. They seemed very nice – the girl smelled friendly, which was important.

The door clicked softly open and Alfie's ears pricked up. It was the girl, Evie. "Sssh!" she murmured. "We mustn't let Mum and Dad hear us, Alfie. You're supposed to stay in your basket, but I bet you're scared down here on your own. I'm taking you up to my bedroom instead. Mrs Wilson said you were very well house-trained, so I'll put some newspaper down for you, OK? Mum would be cross if you weed on my carpet!" She snuggled him close as they crept up the stairs, and Alfie settled into her arms. This was much better than a basket, even a nice one like he'd been given.

Of course, Evie's mum and dad soon worked out exactly what was going on, but they were so glad that Alfie was settling in, and making Evie so happy, that they pretended not to notice. From that night on, Alfie slept on Evie's bed every night, snoring gently.

It didn't take long for Alfie to become part of the family. He was such a friendly little dog. After a couple of weeks, when he'd had all his injections, he was allowed to go out for walks, which meant he could go to school to pick up Evie. She loved coming out to see Mum waiting with Alfie on his bright red lead. Usually it was twisted all round his paws and he tripped over it as he tried to race over to her. Her friends were all really jealous, and Alfie got petted and stroked by everyone. Then they'd head home and Alfie would watch TV with Evie on the sofa. He soon decided on his favourite programmes, and he got very good at singing along to the theme tunes in a tuneful howl.

Mum hadn't been so sure about getting a dog, but Alfie won her over very quickly. He loved people, and he followed her round the house as she did the housework. He was far better company than the radio! And whenever she sat down, he rested his head on her feet.

Of course, Alfie didn't have to work hard to charm Evie's gran. She was always popping over to see him and Evie, and it was great to have her to ask about dog-training tips. It only took Alfie a few days to learn about asking to go outside and Gran warned Evie not to give him too many doggy chocolates as a reward, as he was starting to look a bit tubby!

Once Alfie could meet up with other dogs, Evie took him round to Gran's house to be introduced to Ben and Tigger. Alfie was a little shy at first – they were a lot bigger than he was, especially Tigger – but after half an hour he was chasing them round the garden. Ben the spaniel soon worked out a good way to calm Alfie down when he was being too puppyish and excitable – he sat on him! Evie panicked the first time he did it, but Gran said it would probably be good for Alfie to have an older dog bossing him around, and that Ben wouldn't hurt him.

Evie and Dad soon got into the habit of taking Alfie for an evening walk after dinner. It gave Mum the chance to snooze on the sofa in front of the television. Now that the baby was getting really big, she was tired a lot of the time. Dad and Evie always took a ball with them, or Alfie's favourite, a frisbee. Dad had spotted it in the pet shop and bought it for when Alfie was bigger, but once Alfie saw it, he didn't want to wait. So what if the frisbee was almost as big as he was? He was very good at catching it – he could do massive leaps into mid-air, twisting and turning and snatching the frisbee as it fell. Then he'd haul it over the grass back to Evie, and sit panting exhaustedly for a minute, before yapping for them to throw it again. A couple of times he'd worn himself out so much that Dad had to carry him home and lay the exhausted puppy in his basket. Evie was so happy that Alfie had become part of the family – she couldn't imagine life at home without him now.

Chapter Three

One night, Alfie was curled up snugly in a nest of duvet on top of Evie's toes. He was twitching happily in his sleep, dreaming of breakfast, when he was woken by the sound of Evie's parents talking. He sat up and listened carefully – it wasn't something he expected to hear in the middle of the night. Something interesting was going on. He padded up to the top of the bed, and licked Evie's ear.

"Grrmmpf!" Evie wriggled and wiped the lick off her face. "Alfie! It's the middle of the night, silly, what are you doing?" She yawned, and gave a little stretch. "Go back to sleep. It's ages till we have to get up." Then she turned over and snuggled her face back into her pillow.

Alfie huffed through his nose irritably. Why wouldn't Evie listen? Couldn't she tell that something exciting was happening? He took hold of Evie's pyjama sleeve with his teeth, very, very gently, and pulled.

"OK, Alfie, what is it?" she asked sleepily. "Do you need a wee? Because if you think I'm taking you all round the garden to find a good place at this time of night you can think again!"

Alfie yapped sharply, and tugged at Evie's sleeve again. Then he dropped the sleeve and stood silently, his ears pricked up.

Evie listened, and at last she understood why Alfie was behaving so strangely. Her parents weren't just talking now, they were moving around too. Doors were opening and shutting quietly, and she could hear her dad on the phone to someone, sounding anxious. The baby was coming! It had to be that. Evie pulled her pillow up and leaned back against it, whispering to Alfie to come and sit with her. He burrowed in under her arm and they listened together in the dark. Someone was arriving downstairs.

"That'll be Gran, I bet," Evie murmured. "They said they'd ask her to come and stay with me when they had to go to the hospital."

Alfie grunted in agreement. He liked

Gran. She had dog chocolates in her handbag.

A few minutes later, the front door banged, and they heard someone coming back up the stairs. At last Evie's bedroom door eased open, and Gran popped her head around.

"Hi, Gran!" Evie whispered.

"Hello, darling! I thought you might have woken up, with all the coming and going. I just came to check on you."

"Alfie woke me up. Is Mum having the baby now?" Evie sounded anxious.

Gran perched herself on the end of Evie's bed, and stroked Alfie's nose.

"Clever Alfie. Yes, they think so. Don't get too excited though – these things can take a while." She smiled down at Evie, still cuddling the little dog, and decided that she'd been wrong to worry. Evie loved him so much, and a dog would be just what her granddaughter needed to keep her company over the next few weeks.

The next day Evie's parents brought baby Sam home. Evie's mum and Sam were both doing really well, and they didn't need to stay in hospital. Mum said the noise of all the other babies in the ward was driving her mad, and she wanted to be home in her own bed.

Even though they were coming home as soon as they possibly could, the wait still seemed like ages to Evie.

It was a Saturday, so she was at home, with Alfie and Gran. The day really dragged, even though as a treat they all walked to the fish and chip shop to get lunch. Gran stood outside with Alfie, who was blissfully breathing in the smell of chips, and Evie went in to get their food. When they got back, both Evie and Gran naughtily fed Alfie the odd chip under the table, so he was soon full and fast asleep.

Evie couldn't help listening out for the car – Dad had rung to say they'd be home sometime that afternoon, they just had to wait for a doctor to give Mum one last check. Their road was pretty quiet, but Evie ran to the window to look at least ten times before she finally spotted their car pulling up.

"They're here!" she squeaked. Gran came hurrying over to join Evie. Evie's dad was trying to get the new baby seat out of the car and all they could see of her new brother was a little bit of blue blanket trailing out of the seat.

Alfie couldn't tell what Evie was thinking, which was odd, because usually he had a good idea. Was she happy about this strange new thing that was happening? He licked her hand, and made a questioning little "wuff?" noise.

"That's the baby, Alfie. My brother Sam. Let's go and see." Evie scrambled down from the window sill, and Alfie trotted after her out into the hallway. Gran had opened the door, and Evie's parents were just bringing the baby in.

"Evie!" Mum hugged her tightly. "I missed you. Were you and Gran OK?"

"Of course. Can I see him, Mum?" Evie crouched down next to the baby seat and peered in. Sam seemed tiny inside – just a small hand clenched tightly round the blanket, and a pale little face half-covered by a hat.

"Let's get him in and unwrap him, then you can see him properly. It's a bit chilly outside so he had to be covered up," Mum explained.

Alfie followed interestedly as the family went into the kitchen. The baby smelled new and different, and he wanted to investigate.

Gran and Evie watched as Mum undid Sam's little jacket, with Dad's help. At last she stood up, and carried him over. "Do you want to sit down, Evie?" she asked. "Then you can have a cuddle."

Evie whisked over to a chair and sat down, eagerly holding out her arms.

Mum kissed Sam's nose, and handed him very carefully to Evie. "Sam, this is your big sister!"

Evie sat holding Sam, a look of amazement on her face. "He's smaller than some of my old dolls," she whispered, looking worriedly up at Mum. "Is he all right?"

Dad laughed. "He'll grow. You were littler than that."

Evie gazed down at Sam, watching as his eyes gradually opened. "He's looking straight at me!" she squealed, beaming in delight.

Mum laughed. "I think he is! They say new babies can't really see much, but he's definitely staring at you."

"You know, he looks quite like Evie," Dad put in.

"Yes, I see what you mean," Gran agreed.

Alfie watched as they all chattered excitedly. He was feeling confused. No one had introduced him to the new baby. Evie was his person, and she was ignoring him. He gave a sharp little yap, and everyone jumped. The tiny creature on Evie's lap gasped and let out a shuddering wail that made Alfie back away. What was it?

"Alfie!" Evie said crossly. "What did you have to do that for? Look, you've made Sam cry."

Alfie backed away still further, his
tail tucking between his legs. Now Evie
was cross with him. He wasn't sure he
liked this *baby* thing at all.

Over the next few days, Evie fell in love with her new little brother. Sam didn't do much, except lie in a Moses basket and wail occasionally, but he was very cute. Evie's dad had some time off work to help out, so Evie had tried arguing that she ought to have time off school too, but apparently it didn't work that way. She had to go back to school on Monday morning. Dad dropped her off in the car.

"You will bring Sam to pick me up, won't you?" she begged her mum. "I want everyone to see him. He's so much nicer than anyone else's little brothers and sisters."

The trip to pick up Evie from school was the first time Mum had taken Sam out in his new pushchair. Alfie watched as Dad wrestled with the pushchair. It would be nice to have a walk. He'd been let out in the garden over the weekend, but no one had taken him for a proper run, and he was keen to be out smelling some good smells. Alfie went to fetch his lead – it hung over a hook in the hall, and he could tug it down. He trotted back with it in his mouth just as Mum was manoeuvring the pushchair over the front step.

"You're sure you don't want me to come?" Dad asked again.

"No, you start making the tea, we'll be fine." And she closed the door behind her. Without Alfie!

Alfie barked to remind Mum she'd left him behind – it wasn't like her to forget, but perhaps that baby had distracted her.

"Not today, Alfie." Dad shook his head. "Sorry, boy, but it's a bit much to have you *and* the pushchair." He patted Alfie's head and went back into the kitchen, leaving Alfie in the hall, his lead still trailing out of his mouth.

Alfie stared at the door, confused. He always went to pick Evie up from school. Was Evie's mum really not coming back for him?

"Alfie! Biscuit!"

Evie's dad was calling. Alfie gave the door one last hopeful look. Ah well. He supposed a biscuit was better than nothing…

When Mum and Evie got back from school they were both looking a bit frazzled. Sam had snoozed most of the way, and then woken up just in time for everyone to say how cute he was, but now he was hungry, and cross, and a thin wailing noise was coming from his nest of blankets.

Mum sat on the sofa to feed him, and Evie curled up next to her to watch – she'd really missed seeing Sam while she was at school. Alfie jumped up too – he thought they were going to watch television together, like they usually did. But Evie squeaked in horror and pushed him off. "Alfie, no! You might squash Sam!"

Alfie's tail drooped, and he slunk miserably into the kitchen. The baby was going to watch all his favourite programmes with Evie instead. It wasn't fair.

All the next week, people kept popping round with presents for the new baby, and quite often one for Evie too. Everyone seemed to think Sam was very special, and he got fussed over all the time. Alfie wasn't quite sure why. Sam didn't do a lot, and he certainly couldn't do tricks like a dog could. Alfie couldn't help wishing that things would go back to normal, and everyone would fuss over him instead, but he had a feeling it wasn't going to happen.

But at least Alfie had been able to reclaim his place on the sofa, as Mum said she thought it was OK for Alfie to sit there when she was feeding Sam, as long as Evie was careful not to let Alfie lick him.

"Alfie's used to sitting there with you, Evie," she pointed out. "It isn't fair if he's not allowed to any more. Just keep an eye on him." She sat Sam up to get him to burp, and smiled. "Look, Sam's watching Alfie's tail wag. I should think he'll love having Alfie for company."

Evie scratched Alfie behind the ears, and he settled down on her lap, keeping a watchful eye on the baby. He supposed he didn't mind sharing the sofa.

Chapter Four

"Evie! Evie! You're going to be late for school!" Mum was calling up the stairs, sounding cross. She had Sam tucked under one arm, and he was grizzling too. "You won't have time for breakfast!"

Evie stomped down the stairs looking very gloomy. "I don't want any. And I don't want to go to school either. I don't feel very well. I'm really tired."

Evie's mum took a deep breath and counted to five. "I know. We all are. But it's Friday, you can sleep in over the weekend."

"If Sam doesn't keep me awake all night, like he did last night," Evie growled.

"It's not his fault, Evie, he doesn't understand the difference between night and day yet." Mum was sounding really strained.

"Well, can't you teach him?" Evie looked up at her mum and suddenly grinned. "Oh, all right. I suppose not. But I am really, really tired." She sighed and hooked her finger into Sam's tiny hand. "Don't you dare nap all afternoon, Sam. Stay up and then you'll sleep tonight!"

It hadn't been a good week. Evie's dad was back at work now, and it was harder to get everything done without the extra help. Sam was gorgeous, but he wasn't sleeping well, and when he was awake he was loud. Everyone's temper was fraying.

Alfie was trying his best to keep out of the way, but he never managed to be in the right place. Most days Evie's mum walked into him about three times just doing the washing-up. When she got back from taking Evie to school that Friday, she tripped over Alfie while she was carrying a basket of washing, and trod on his paw, but she didn't seem to be sorry. He held it up and whined, but all she did was snap, "Alfie! Not again! Get out of the way,

61

you silly dog!" Alfie limped out of the kitchen, feeling very hard done by.

He sat in the hallway, thoughtfully chewing on a small teddy bear he'd found on the stairs. He just couldn't seem to do anything right any more. Things had been much nicer before.

At that moment, Sam started crying upstairs and Mum dashed past to go and fetch him – and saw the small pile of shredded fur that had once been a teddy. "Alfie!" she wailed, and Alfie gazed up at her. He didn't know why she was cross – furry toys were there to be chewed, and he didn't see what the fuss was about. But it looked like Mum didn't agree, judging by the way she snatched up what was left of the teddy and glared at him.

Alfie was still in disgrace when Gran popped round that afternoon, and he was delighted to see her. At last someone who actually had time to sit and scratch him behind the ears properly! He leaned against Gran's leg affectionately. For a moment he almost wished that she would take him back to her house. Then he shook his head and snorted. No! He was Evie's dog. He was sure that she would get over the baby thing soon, and then maybe they could go back to proper walks and more cuddling.

"You look exhausted!" Gran was saying to Mum. "Why don't you pop upstairs and have a nap? I'll look after Sam for you."

Mum sighed. "I'd love to, but he's being so grumpy today. He wouldn't even go to his dad this morning – every time I put him down he howls. I just don't know what's the matter with him. Anyway, I've got to go and fetch Evie in a minute."

Gran stood up firmly. "There you are then. Put him in the pushchair and I'll take him with me and get Evie for you. You go and have a rest. Sam will probably sleep too."

"If you're sure…" Mum tucked Sam in, and set off upstairs, looking grateful.

Me too! Me too! Alfie whined hopefully, bouncing round Gran's ankles as she headed for the door. He was still desperate for more walks.

"Sorry, Alfie, I'd love to take you, but I'm not used to this pushchair and I can't manage both of you." She looked down at the little dog thoughtfully. "I'd better talk to Evie about you. I don't think she's exercising you enough."

Alfie yelped in agreement, and she nodded to herself.

Unfortunately, Gran's master plan for settling Sam didn't work. At five o'clock, when she had to leave to go and get Tigger and Ben their tea, Sam was still wailing. And when Evie's dad walked in at six, he was greeted by a howling baby, a frazzled wife and a cross daughter.

"Looks like we're in for a fun weekend," he joked, but nobody else thought it was funny.

Alfie watched Dad hopefully. Mum and Evie had been so stressed by Sam's crying that they had forgotten to feed him. He nosed eagerly at his food bowl, and looked up at Dad. He wasn't watching. Alfie sighed and trailed back to his basket, where he curled up with his back to the rest of the family. Maybe he'd better just have a sleep and try again in a bit.

A couple of hours later, Alfie was convinced he was going to starve if he didn't get fed soon. He trotted into the living room, where Mum and Dad were taking turns to walk Sam up and down. Evie was just getting ready to go up to bed. Alfie was horrified. If Evie went to bed, they'd never remember to feed him! Desperate measures were needed. He nipped back to the kitchen.

"Oh, thank goodness," Mum murmured, watching as Sam slumped slightly on his dad's shoulder. "He's going off to sleep. No, don't stop!"

Dad nodded grimly, and resumed his trek up and down the room. "I think he's fallen asleep," he sighed, a couple of minutes later. "Can we risk laying him down, do you—"

It was at that moment that Alfie trotted back in, carrying his metal food bowl in his teeth. He dropped it hard on the wooden floor, and barked.

Sam shot upright and let out a blood-curdling wail.

"Alfie! You bad dog!" Mum groaned. "That's it. Kitchen! Now! In your basket!" And she shooed him out, flapping her hands crossly.

Alfie was banished. It was the first night he'd ever spent in the kitchen, instead of curled up on the end of Evie's bed. He was so confused. He'd only wanted his tea! Everyone else had had theirs, and he was starving.

For the next hour, Alfie and Sam howled together. Then Sam suddenly decided not to bother any more and fell blissfully asleep; but Alfie lay in his basket, and stared at the dark kitchen. Why didn't Evie want him upstairs? What had he done?

Didn't she love him any more?

Chapter Five

The next morning was Saturday, and the family was having breakfast. It was always a really nice time – the beginning of the weekend, when they all had a chance to relax. They usually had something extra-nice for breakfast too. Today, not even croissants could cheer everyone up.

At least Sam seemed to be in a better

mood. He was lying in his bouncy chair in the living room.

"He's fine," Dad reported back after a quick check. "Seems to be enjoying himself actually – I think he's learning to bat at that dangly toy you bought him, Evie." He gave a long, slow sigh of relief, sat down and poured himself a large cup of coffee.

Alfie jumped up, his paws on Dad's knee, holding his squeaky bone hopefully in his mouth. Dad was usually good for a game.

"Not now, Alfie," Dad muttered, pushing him away gently.

Alfie went to paw at Evie's ankles, hoping for a bit of croissant. She dangled a piece by his nose, and he gulped it down gratefully.

"Evie!" Mum said sharply. "Are you giving Alfie scraps? How many times have I told you not to feed that dog at the table?" Mum didn't normally mind that much, but today she was tired and snappish.

"Shoo, Alfie!" Evie whispered, nudging him out from under the table with her foot.

Alfie took one look at Mum's cross face, and trailed sadly into the living room. He sat down next to Sam. The baby was half-smiling at the bouncy animals toy stretched across the front of his chair, and vaguely waving a hand at it every so often. Alfie watched. It was quite fun. He lay down with his nose on his paws and gazed up as the little creatures jumped and danced.

Sam smelled nice – milky – and he was relaxing to be with after the tense, grumpy mood in the kitchen. Sam made little squeaky, grunting noises to himself, and Alfie wuffed quietly back, his eyes slowly closing as he drifted off for a snooze.

After a few minutes, the jingling of the toy was joined by an irritating buzz. Alfie opened one eye. Was it Sam making that noise? Was he supposed to do that? No, Sam was asleep. The buzzing was from a large fly that had landed on the baby's arm. Alfie bristled as he watched it crawl over Sam. He hated flies, and he knew Evie's mum did too, if ever a fly buzzed near she always shooed it away. That fly should *not* be crawling over Sam.

Alfie watched, waiting for his moment to pounce. He was so intent on the fly, that he had no idea Evie and her mum had come into the living room to check on Sam. They watched in horror as Alfie pounced, his sharp white teeth snapping on the fly – just millimetres away from Sam's arm.

"Alfie, no!" Evie screamed, as her mum threw herself forward to grab Sam away.

Alfie had never heard Evie sound like that before – terrified and angry at the same time. He shot under the sofa and lay there cowering.

Sam hadn't noticed the fly, but he certainly noticed when his mum snatched him out of his nice sleep. He roared angrily, and waved his arms about.

"Mum, is he OK? I can't believe Alfie tried to bite him!" Tears were rolling down Evie's cheeks.

Evie's mum was breathing fast – from where she and Evie had been standing, it really had looked as though Alfie had meant to bite Sam's arm, and she'd been terrified. She was pushing up the sleeve of his sleepsuit, searching for marks, but he seemed fine – just cross at being woken.

"What happened? Are you all right?" Evie's dad rushed into the room, dressing gown flapping. "Is something the matter with Sam?" he asked, taking in the scene.

"No. No, we're all OK," Evie's mum said slowly.

"Dad, Alfie nearly bit Sam!" Evie sobbed, throwing her arms around him. She couldn't believe that her lovely puppy would do such a horrible thing – but then she'd seen it with her own eyes and watched him jump at her baby brother, teeth bared.

"I don't think he did, Evie." Mum

sounded as though she was trying to work it all out. "Look."

Lying on the floor next to the bouncy chair was a huge bluebottle, legs in the air, still buzzing faintly.

"You know how Alfie hates flies, he's always snapping at them. I think he just tried to catch a fly that had landed on Sam's arm."

Evie lifted her head from where it was buried in her dad's dressing gown. "Really?"

Evie's dad was looking serious. "Are you sure?"

"Well, no, I suppose not. But Alfie's never done anything like that before, has he?"

Evie shook her head, smiling in relief. "Never! Oh, Mum, thank goodness you saw that fly – we'd never have known otherwise."

"Where is Alfie?" Dad asked, looking round.

"I shouted at him and he disappeared under the sofa!" Evie went pale. "Oh, he must think we're so angry! Poor Alfie." Evie crouched down to look, but Alfie flinched away from her, and retreated right to the back. Evie sat up, looking hurt. "He won't come," she said miserably.

"You probably need to give him a bit of time." Dad put an arm round her, and the other round Mum and Sam. "Come on into the kitchen."

Alfie huddled under the sofa, trembling. No one had ever shouted at him like that before. Evie had behaved as though he'd done something terrible. But he'd been helping Sam! Evie's mum was always saying that flies were horrible, dirty things. She waved them away if they got anywhere near the baby. *Did Evie and Mum think I was trying to bite Sam?* Alfie wondered. *I'd never do that! Don't they know I'd never do that?* Alfie lay there, feeling confused. No one seemed to understand him very much here any more. He was always in trouble, and even Evie, who used to love him so much, didn't seem to have any time for him. Maybe they really did think he was the sort of dog who would bite.

"Alfie! Alfie!" Evie was calling him. She was lying down, peering under the sofa. "Come out, Alfie, please? I didn't mean it. Please come out, I'm so sorry for shouting at you." Her eyes met his hopefully, and Alfie couldn't hold back any longer.

He crept forward, tail slowly starting to wag. As he wriggled out from under the sofa, she hugged him tight, burying her face in his thick white fur. "Oh, Alfie." Alfie put his paws on her shoulders and licked her face, tasting salt from her tears. Why was she crying? Everything was all right now. He wagged his tail, and licked her again lovingly.

"Uuurgh, Alfie..." Evie giggled and sniffed. "I'm covered in lick. Oh, I do love you." She sighed. "I'm so sorry. I haven't been showing it much, have I?"

Alfie wuffed encouragingly. He adored Evie, and he trusted her. Hearing the love in Evie's voice as he snuggled against her was all he needed to feel better.

Chapter Six

The rest of the day was almost perfect for Alfie. Evie seemed to be back to her old self. She cuddled him loads, and she kept saying she was sorry for thinking he'd hurt Sam, and telling him what a clever dog he was for catching the fly. Just every so often, Alfie would remember how upset and angry everyone had been, and shudder, and then Evie would hug him all over again.

Only one thing spoilt it. Alfie kept catching worried looks between Evie's mum and dad – worried looks directed at him. Maybe they thought he might still be frightened, he wondered. He tried to be extra bouncy and friendly, with lots of jumping up to lick them, but it didn't seem to work. If anything, they looked more worried, although they always patted him and smiled.

Evie gave him a huge tea and Alfie was so full afterwards that he went to sleep on her lap while she was trying to finish off her homework at the kitchen table. He didn't notice Evie's parents come to sit with her, or see the anxious looks on their faces.

"Evie." Mum sounded strangely nervous. "Evie, we have to talk to you, sweetheart."

Evie looked up. "I'm doing it! Look, I'm doing it now. It's only Saturday, Mum, I'll get it done, easily!"

"Not about your homework." Dad's voice was really flat, and Evie looked at him, suddenly scared. This was far more serious than just them complaining that she was rushing through her homework at the last minute.

"It's about Alfie," Dad went on.

Her heart suddenly thumping, Evie put her hand down to stroke Alfie, curled on her lap. He gave a little whine of pleasure, and stretched out luxuriously in his sleep before curling himself up again even tighter. "What's the matter?" Evie asked quietly.

Her mum and dad exchanged a look, then her dad sighed. "We're not sure we can keep him, Evie."

Evie gulped, her hand tightening on Alfie's neck so that he wriggled uncomfortably. "Why?" she whispered. Then her voice strengthened. "He wasn't biting, Dad, really," she assured him. "He wouldn't do that." She smiled desperately at her dad, knowing she had to convince him.

"Evie, you thought he would," Dad said gently. "And so did your mum. You were so upset this morning."

"But he didn't! It was all a mistake." Evie's eyes were filling with tears. Her dad sounded so decided. She turned to her mum for help, and saw that she was crying too.

"It's not Alfie's fault at all. It's just that we haven't been able to look after Alfie properly, Evie," her mum said shakily. "We all love him, but he needs proper walks, and lots of attention. He hasn't been getting that. Dogs can get very grumpy if they're cooped up in the house all day."

"I'll walk him more!" Evie cried out. "Every day! Twice a day. I've just been taken up with having Sam around, that's all."

"We all have," her dad agreed. "But that's not fair on Alfie – he needs a home where he doesn't get forgotten about."

"I didn't mean to!" Evie wailed, so loudly that Alfie woke up, his little white head suddenly popping up at the table, making them all giggle hopelessly. He gave them a happy, doggy smile, showing lots of long pink tongue. What was the joke? Then he looked again, turning to sniff at Evie. Maybe there wasn't a joke at all. Something felt wrong. Had he done something bad again? He hunched down on to Evie's lap, looking scared.

"Evie, look at him. He's upset. It's not fair to put him through that," Evie's mum said gently.

Evie sniffed. "If – if we're not going to keep him, what are we going to do? Are you going to give him back to Mrs Wilson?" She gulped, imagining Alfie sitting sadly in the puppy room all on his own, his brother and sisters already gone to new homes.

"No." Dad looked thoughtful. "It would have been the best option, but she's stopped breeding dogs now. She's retired to the seaside, remember?"

"I suppose she might take just Alfie back…" Mum said. "Oh, but we don't have her new address."

"I think the sensible thing would be to take him to Riverside," Dad said firmly, as though he was trying to convince himself.

"Riverside?" Evie's eyes filled with tears again. "Where Gran got Ben and Tigger? But that's for dogs that people don't want! We *do* want Alfie!"

"Dogs that people can't keep, Evie." Mum's voice sounded so sorry that Evie knew there was no point arguing. Hugging Alfie to her, she jumped up and raced up the stairs to her room.

Evie didn't come down for dinner. Alfie had already had his huge tea, and he was delighted to stay upstairs with Evie all evening. She was paying him loads of attention, teasing and tickling him, and playing all his favourite games. At bedtime he was allowed to snuggle up on her bed again. Alfie heaved a deep, happy sigh. This was where he was meant to be, not down in the kitchen on his own. Everything was the way it should be. He fell asleep at once, worn out from all the playing – so he didn't notice that Evie lay awake half the night, tears rolling silently down her cheeks.

"Evie, you don't have to come."

Alfie looked interestedly back and forth between Evie and Dad. They were going somewhere! Excellent! He pattered off to fetch his lead, and jumped up with his paws on Evie's knees to give it to her.

Evie gulped, and tears started to seep from the corners of her eyes again. He was such a lovely dog! How could they be doing this? Hurriedly she wiped the tears away – she didn't want Alfie to know what was going on. "I'm coming," she said firmly, her voice hardly shaking at all. "I'm not having Alfie think I didn't say goodbye."

Dad sighed. "OK. Hey, Alfie, come on, boy. You're going on a car ride," he said, trying to sound cheerful.

But Alfie laid his ears back. Something odd was going on. He jumped into the car and saw that Evie's hands were trembling as she did up his harness. Usually Evie would beg her dad to have the radio on and they'd sing along, but today they hardly spoke at all.

When the car stopped, Alfie thought Evie would put his lead on and let him walk, but for some reason she was carrying him up in front of her so she could nuzzle into his fur. Alfie licked her face gratefully. He liked being carried, so he could see what was going on. Evie was walking very slowly though – Dad kept stopping and looking back for her as they headed towards the building. Alfie wasn't surprised. It didn't smell good, too clean, a bit like the vet's that he'd been taken to a few weeks before.

What was this place?

Evie stood by the reception desk, while Dad explained quietly to a girl in a green uniform. She was nodding sympathetically, and she gave Alfie a considering look.

"I'm sure he'll be rehomed very quickly. He's a lovely little dog." She came round the reception desk and held out her arms. "Come on, sweetie," she crooned to Alfie.

Alfie felt suddenly scared. Who was this girl? Why were they here? All at once he knew that the lovely, cuddly time he'd been having with Evie over the last day hadn't been real. In fact, nothing had been right since he'd snapped at that fly on Sam's arm. But he still didn't understand! What should he have done? He scrabbled helplessly as the girl in green lifted him from Evie's arms. He was squealing with fright, desperately trying to get away.

"Come on, Evie." Her dad quickly marched Evie away, before she grabbed Alfie back again. Alfie's last sight of Evie was as her dad hustled her out of the door, hugging her tightly against him, so that she couldn't turn and see her little dog howling for her to come back.

Chapter Seven

As Evie trailed up the front path, she heard someone calling her, and excited woofs. She spun round immediately, thinking that somehow it was Alfie.

"Hello, Evie! Ben and Tigger and I are just out for our walk. We thought we'd see if you and Alfie wanted to come with us. I know you haven't had a lot of time to walk him recently."

Gran was beaming at Evie, but then she noticed Evie's dad, who was shaking his head and holding his finger to lips.

"Jack, are you all right?" Gran asked worriedly, as Tigger and Ben towed her through the gate.

Evie's dad sighed. "Not really."

Evie crouched down to pat Ben and Tigger. "We just took Alfie to Riverside," she told them quietly. Somehow it was easier to tell the dogs than Gran. Suddenly she remembered. "You were right, Gran, you said we wouldn't be able to manage."

"Oh, sweetheart, I'm really sorry." Gran's face crumpled. "I hadn't realized it was that bad. Why didn't you say?" she asked Evie's dad.

He shrugged. "It was one of those difficult decisions…" he said sadly. "I'm sure someone really nice will take Alfie home. You know that, Evie, don't you?"

Evie was fighting back tears. She didn't want anybody else taking Alfie anywhere, even if they fed him out of a solid gold bowl! He was her dog – only he wasn't. Not any more. In fact, she suddenly realized, she was never going to see him again. She gasped, and then she scrambled up and dashed into the house, tears stinging her eyes.

"That little Westie's still not eating."

"Really? He's only been here three days. He'll change his mind soon."

The two girls in the green Riverside uniform leaned against the wall, sipping their tea, and staring thoughtfully into Alfie's run. He was curled up at the back, a miserable little ball, not even looking at his overflowing food bowl.

"He's really taking it hard, poor little thing."

"Yeah, I was here when they brought him in – the little girl he belonged to was really upset too."

Alfie snuggled his paws further round his ears to shut out their voices. If he kept his eyes shut tight, he could almost pretend that he was back home.

"Alfie! Alfie!"

Alfie twitched, but it wasn't Evie. It was another of the Riverside staff, with some people looking for a dog. Quite a few people had been to see Alfie already, and everyone said how cute he was. They seemed surprised, as though such a sweet puppy shouldn't really be at a dogs' home. But when they tried to talk to Alfie, and he refused to budge from the back of his run, they gave up, moving on to friendlier dogs.

"Mum, look at this great dog!" A boy about Evie's age was peering through the fence. "Can we meet him? Please?"

"Sure." The Riverside girl got out her keys. "This is Alfie. He's a gorgeous Westie puppy who is being rehomed because his owners had a new baby and couldn't keep him. He's a lovely boy, but he's not too happy right now. Hey, Alfie..." She cooed gently to him. "Come and meet Ethan, he's looking for a nice dog just like you."

Alfie hunched himself up tighter. The staff at Riverside were right. He hadn't accepted what was going on. How could he? He didn't understand. He couldn't let anyone take him home, because Evie was coming back for him. He was sure of it. But he was becoming just a little less sure every time he woke up and he was still in a grey concrete run, waiting for her.

The girl picked him up, and Alfie lay limply and sadly in her arms as she carried him out. The little boy stroked him gently. "He's great."

Ethan's eyes were shining, just like Evie's used to. Alfie let Ethan scratch him behind the ears. That was nice.

"Can we take him home?" Ethan begged.

Home! Alfie suddenly twisted in the Riverside girl's arms, and growled angrily. What was he thinking? His home was with Evie.

Ethan's parents pulled him away quickly to look at another dog, and the girl with the keys sighed. "Oh, Alfie. That would have been a wonderful home. When are you going to give up and let someone else love you?"

Alfie slunk back into his run, and curled up facing the wall. He only wanted *Evie* to love him.

Evie thought it was strange that her house could feel so different, just because Alfie wasn't there. She didn't have a warm body curled on her toes at night. No cold nose was resting on her knee at mealtimes, hoping for scraps. Only Mum and Sam met her from school, and she and Dad didn't go for walks any more. Alfie going had changed everything.

She tried to explain to Gran when she went round after school on Wednesday.

"I never really thought how nice it was having Alfie to play with when Mum was busy. She's got so much to do with feeding Sam, and everything. But I had Alfie, and it was OK. I really miss him, Gran." She stared into her juice, and Tigger pushed his head into her lap, sensing that she was unhappy. "Yeah, you miss him too, don't you, Tigger?"

"I should think your parents miss Alfie as well, you know," Gran said.

Evie nodded miserably. "I think Dad does. I caught him in the hall yesterday with Alfie's lead. He looked really confused, and he muttered something about having forgotten. We sometimes used to take Alfie for walks after tea."

"Why don't you talk to them about

it? You might have made the wrong decision." Gran looked thoughtfully at Evie, wondering what she'd say.

Evie stroked Tigger. Then she looked up, and her face was so sad that Gran caught her breath. "I shouldn't ever have let him go, Gran!" She got up to put on her coat. "I miss Alfie so much."

Gran nodded firmly. "I definitely think you should talk to them." She watched Evie walking slowly down the path, and then looked down at Ben and Tigger. They stared back at her encouragingly. "Mmm. Yes, I think you're right," Gran muttered to herself.

A couple of times during the week, Evie thought about what Gran had said, but there didn't seem any point in talking to Mum and Dad about Alfie. It would just make everything worse when they said no, and she was sure she wouldn't be able to change their minds. Then on Saturday morning she wandered into the kitchen, and found her mum staring at something on the table, with a funny look on her face.

"What's the matter?" Evie leaned over to see what she was looking at, and saw that her mum was holding a photo of Alfie.

"Oh! Evie, I didn't hear you come in." Mum quickly put the photo back on the window sill, but Evie was staring at her.

"You miss him too, don't you?" she asked, her voice suddenly full of hope. "Gran said you did, but I didn't believe her." Then her shoulders slumped. "But I suppose it doesn't make any difference." She looked over at Sam, who was sitting in his bouncy chair staring in wonder at his toes. She still adored her baby brother, but she couldn't help thinking that it was his fault.

Mum looked too. "Maybe." Then her voice changed. "Maybe not, Evie. Perhaps we were being too hard on him."

"Who?" Dad walked in with the newspaper. "Got you some chocolate, Evie," he added, throwing her a bar.

Evie caught it automatically, but

didn't even look to see what sort it was. "Dad, Mum thinks maybe we shouldn't have taken Alfie to Riverside!"

Her dad sat down at the table slowly, looking back and forth between them. "Really?" he said thoughtfully.

Mum sat down too. "Come on. Tell me you haven't missed him."

"But that's not the point! We weren't able to look after him properly. And what about Sam? Think back to this time last week!"

"I think we overreacted. We panicked – we were all tired, and we made a snap decision. I don't think it was a good one." Mum reached out for his hand. "Alfie was such fun to have around. Do you really think he would have harmed Sam?"

Evie watched hopefully, holding her breath as Dad shook his head. "To be honest, I think watching Alfie cheered the little guy up sometimes," he said.

They looked over at Sam, who stared back seriously, and said, "Ooooo," in a meaningful way, waving his foot.

"And I really missed taking him to the paper shop this morning," Dad added. "You know, I never came out of the shop and found Alfie on his own – he was always being fussed over by someone. Everyone loved him."

Evie took a deep breath. "So can we go and get him back?" she asked, twisting her fingers together anxiously.

Dad looked serious. "It wasn't just about Sam though, Evie. We'd need to look after Alfie better." He exchanged a glance with Mum. "We need to think this through."

Mum nodded. "Evie, could you do me a big favour and change Sam's nappy?"

"Now?" Evie sounded disbelieving.

"Yes, now." Mum smiled at her. "Your dad and I need to talk. And Sam could do with a nappy change."

Evie picked Sam up, making a face, and carried him upstairs.

When Evie got back, Mum and Dad were looking at the photo of Alfie again. "Have you decided?" Evie asked hopefully, cuddling Sam close.

"Do you think we can all be better owners for Alfie this time round?" Dad asked.

"Yes! And Gran would help!" Evie reminded him. "She said she would. I could take him out for walks with her and Ben and Tigger."

"No getting grumpy with Alfie just because Sam's made us tired."

"No! I promise. Pleeeaaase! Can we have him back?"

Dad grinned at her. "OK. Let's go and get Alfie!"

Evie and her parents were talking excitedly in the car about how great it would be to have Alfie back, when Dad suddenly stopped in the middle of his favourite story about Alfie trying to catch a pigeon.

"I've just thought," he said quietly. "It's possible someone else has already given Alfie a new home. He's been at Riverside a week – and he's such a beautiful dog. Evie, I don't want to upset you, but it's possible Alfie's gone."

Evie gulped. "Can you drive faster?"

Evie and her dad jumped out of the car as soon as they got to the dogs' home, while Mum wrestled with Sam and the pushchair. "You go!" she said, waving them on.

They dashed into Reception, and Dad explained why they had come back, while Evie hopped up and down impatiently. The girl at the desk was taking so long to bring up Alfie's file on the computer. At last Evie couldn't stand it. She slipped through the big double door that led to the dogs' runs. She had to tell Alfie he was coming home!

But Alfie wasn't there.

Chapter Eight

"And they wouldn't tell you who'd taken him?" Mum asked indignantly.

"Well, no. I can see why not. We gave Alfie up. It wouldn't be fair on his new owners if we could just storm round and take him back," Dad pointed out.

Mum sighed. "I suppose not. But it seems so unfair."

"Can we not talk about it?" came a small voice from the backseat. Evie was sadly dangling a toy in front of Sam's car seat, and he was giggling, the only member of the family feeling cheerful.

"Sorry, Evie. You're right, it's not going to change anything. At least we're going to Gran's for tea – that'll make us feel better. I'll bet she's made a cake."

Evie stared at the car ceiling, concentrating on not snapping at her parents. They were only trying to be nice – but honestly, a cake? That was supposed to make it all right that she'd just lost her gorgeous dog for ever? Evie sniffed hard. She didn't want to start crying again, she'd only just managed to stop, and her eyes were hurting. She adored Gran, but she wished they weren't going to her house today. Gran would never have let anything like this happen to Ben or Tigger, and seeing them was just going to make Evie miss Alfie more.

He'll be with a lovely family, she told herself firmly. He'll be having a great time. The Riverside people wouldn't give him to anyone who wouldn't look after him. Someone like us, she couldn't help adding.

Evie had never noticed how many dogs lived in the few streets between her house and Gran's, but that afternoon they seemed to be everywhere. As they turned the corner into Gran's road, she could hear excited yapping, and something tugged in her stomach. It sounded just like Alfie. But it was only Ben and Tigger, playing in the front garden. Gran let them out there sometimes for a change.

Dad put his arm round Evie's shoulders. "You can still come and play with these two, you know," he said sympathetically.

Evie nodded. But it wasn't the same as having her own dog. Although she'd never noticed before how much Ben sounded like Alfie. It was weird that he had that same squeaky bark. Actually, he probably didn't – she was just going to imagine Alfie everywhere for a while. *I wonder how long that will last?* Evie thought to herself miserably. *Ages, I suppose.* She leaned over the gate to undo the latch and the dogs bounded over to say hello.

All three of them.

"Alfie!" Evie gasped, finally realizing that the squeaky bark sounded like Alfie because it *was* Alfie. It was Alfie jumping twice his own height to try to get over the gate to greet her. "Alfie!" She fought with the latch, but she was crying so much that Dad had to open it for her. Alfie shot into her arms and tried to lick her all over, his woofs getting squeakier than ever with excitement.

You came back! You came back! he was saying delightedly, if Evie could have understood him.

"I don't understand," Evie said dazedly, as they sat round the tea-table. Mum had been right, there was a gorgeous-looking cake, although at the moment only Alfie seemed interested in it. He was perched on Evie's knee, gradually easing himself closer and closer to one of the delicious chocolatey bits.

Gran smiled. "Well, after I talked to you, Evie, I changed my mind. I hadn't thought you were ready to have a dog – it's such a huge responsibility. But then with Alfie gone, you seemed so sad. And I love Alfie too. I decided that even if you didn't feel you could have him back right now, with Sam so little, then I would keep him myself and you could visit him. Ben and Tigger like having a bouncy young dog to cheer them up." She looked over at her dogs, who were slumped exhaustedly on their cushions. Tigger seemed to have his paws over his eyes. "Mmmm. Well, the extra exercise is good for them."

"We can take him home, can't we? He can live with us, like Gran said. And Gran can help us out if we're having a problem?" Evie asked her parents anxiously.

"Definitely!" said her dad. "Alfie's part of the family. Aren't you, boy?" Then he laughed. "And Sam thinks so too."

Sam was sitting on Mum's lap, next to Evie and Alfie. He was leaning over towards Alfie, his fingers clumsily batting at Alfie's shiny collar tag, so that it jingled and flashed in the sun. Sam gurgled happily, enjoying his game. Alfie shook his ears and snorted gently, edging slightly closer on Evie's knee so Sam could reach.

Evie smiled down at him, hugging him tightly. Alfie knew that he was home for good.

Out Now:

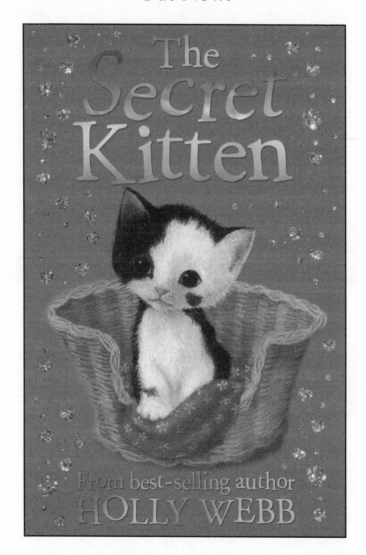

The Secret Kitten

From best-selling author HOLLY WEBB

Out Now:

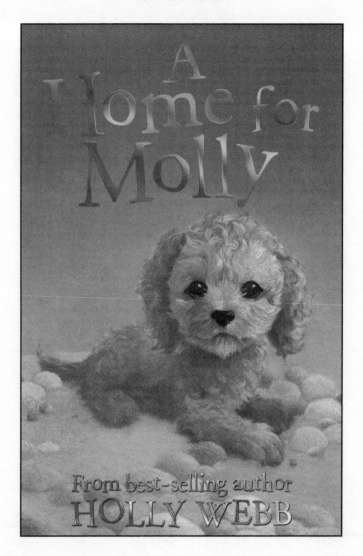

A Home for Molly

From best-selling author
HOLLY WEBB

HOLLY WEBB

Holly Webb started out as a children's book editor, and wrote her first series for the publisher she worked for. She has been writing ever since, with over one hundred books to her name. Holly lives in Berkshire, with her husband and three young sons. Holly's pet cats are always nosying around when she is trying to type on her laptop.

For more information
about Holly Webb visit:

www.holly-webb.com